Little Kangaroo
Finds His Way

Ariane Chottin
Adapted by Patricia Jensen
Illustrations by Catherine Fichaux

Reader's Digest Kids
Pleasantville, N.Y.— Montreal

One summer, the river dried up. The kangaroos didn't have enough water or food.

"We are in great danger," said Grandfather Kangaroo. "One of us must go to the Wise Lizard. She will know what to do."

"But who will go?" asked Grandmother. "We are all needed here to take care of the babies and search for food and water."

Mother Kangaroo spoke up. "I think my son is old enough to make the trip." She turned to Little Kangaroo and asked, "Will you go for us?"

Little Kangaroo nodded and tried to look brave.

The next day, Little Kangaroo stood at the edge of the deep forest. "I want to help my family," he thought, "but I am scared. What if I get lost?"

Little Kangaroo tried to remember the directions he had been given. "The Wise Lizard lives somewhere beyond the forest."

Little Kangaroo saw a path through the trees. He took a deep breath and set out.

Little Kangaroo followed the path through the forest. On the far side, he found flat, open land. First he hopped in one direction. Then he tried another direction. He didn't know where to go.

"Yoo hoo!" called a large owl. "Do you need some help?"

"Yes," said Little Kangaroo. "I must find the way to the Wise Lizard. It's very important."

"You're quite young to be making such a long trip," said the owl. "I will help you." The owl nodded to his left. "Go in that direction until you come to a stream."

Little Kangaroo followed the owl's advice. Finally, he reached a wide stream and sat down at the edge of the water.

"I don't know where to go next," he thought. Tears filled his eyes as he looked up and down the stream. "I'm lost!" he cried.

"Z-z-z-z. Where are you going?" buzzed a large, fuzzy bee.

"I'm looking for the Wise Lizard," said Little Kangaroo. "I need her advice."

"You're very young to make such a long trip," said the bee. "I will help you. The Wise Lizard lives on the other side of the stream."

"But how will I get across?" asked Little Kangaroo. "The water looks too deep."

"I'll show you the best place to cross," said the bee. "It's easy."

Following the bee's directions, Little Kangaroo leaped across the stream.

"Where are you going in such a hurry?" asked a bright green caterpillar.

Little Kangaroo explained, "I have an important question to ask the Wise Lizard."

"The Wise Lizard!" said the caterpillar. "I've always wanted to see her, but I could never travel that far. My legs aren't long and strong like yours."

"I'll carry you," offered Little Kangaroo. "And you can show me how to get there."

"I think I know the way," said the caterpillar. "Let's try it."

The new friends crossed a wide, grassy valley.
The caterpillar looked around and began to worry.

"I'm afraid we're lost," he said. "I thought the
Wise Lizard would be here, but I don't see her
anywhere. Do you?"

"I don't see anything except those two fat baobab trees," said Little Kangaroo.

"Baobab trees!" said the caterpillar. "This *is* the right place! I know the Wise Lizard lives somewhere near two big baobab trees. Let's keep going."

A few minutes later, Little Kangaroo shouted excitedly, "Do you see that?"

Sitting on a high rock was the Wise Lizard. Little Kangaroo joined the other animals standing near the rock.

The Wise Lizard noticed the young kangaroo right away. "Where have you come from?" she asked in a kind voice.

"From far, far away, where the river has dried up," said Little Kangaroo. "We're running out of food and water. I'm here to ask for your advice."

"You are very brave to have made such a long journey all by yourself," the Wise Lizard told Little Kangaroo. "How did you do it?"

Little Kangaroo thought for a moment. "At first I didn't believe I could," he said. "But I kept trying, and the owl, the bee, and the caterpillar helped me along the way."

The Wise Lizard nodded. "You've done very well," she said. "So take this advice back to the other kangaroos. Tell them to walk toward the mountains until they come to a large lake. There they will find enough water and food."

Little Kangaroo thanked the Wise Lizard and carried his friend the caterpillar back to the stream. Then Little Kangaroo hurried all the way home.

"Look who's here!" shouted the other kangaroos. They gathered around Little Kangaroo, happy to see him safe and sound.

"I knew you could do it," whispered his mother. "And now you know it, too."

As the sun rose early the next morning, the kangaroos set out to find their new home. They all hopped along merrily, but no one felt more joy than Little Kangaroo.

Kangaroo babies, called joeys, are tiny at birth. A joey continues to grow in its mother's pouch for the first few months of life.

The kangaroo moves from place to place by jumping. It can often cover 10 feet in one jump! Its powerful tail is used for balance.

Kangaroos are skillful fighters. They fight by grabbing or pushing with their forepaws and kicking with their hind legs.